CHAPTER ONE
IT'S GONE

DOTTIE PLUM liked to be first at everything.

She liked that her birthday was on the first day of January.

She liked that she lived at Number One Daisy Lane.

And on October first, she liked that she was the first on her block to get a pumpkin.

"First pumpkin," Dottie said proudly, as she set her pumpkin on the first step in front of her house.

It was a perfect pumpkin. And Dottie Plum was happy.

But Dottie wasn't happy when her pumpkin was the first to disappear.

The first thing Dottie did was call her best friend, Casey Calendar. Casey was the perfect person to call when something went wrong, because she always had good ideas for what to do next.

"My pumpkin's gone," Dottie told Casey over the phone.

It took ten seconds for Casey to get to Dottie's house. That was because Casey Calendar lived next door.

The first thing Dottie and Casey did was call Leon Spector. Leon was Dottie and Casey's other best friend.

Leon's house was on the other side of Casey's. But it took him longer than ten seconds to come over because Leon stopped a lot to look at the ground.

Leon was a collector. His current collection was of rocks that were shaped like states. Leon hoped to collect a rock for each one of the fifty states in the United States of America. He hoped to make a whole map of rocks.

Every night before he went to bed, Leon

laid out all the rocks he'd collected so far. He
carefully arranged them on his desk, as if
each rock was a puzzle piece in a big map.

Leon's mother put away the rocks every
morning after he went to school. She
wasn't interested in maps, and she liked
Leon's room to look tidy.

Leon didn't mind that he had to put each
rock back in its right place every night. He
liked working on his map. But most of all,
he liked finding rocks.

Looking for perfect rocks took a lot of

time. That's why Leon was often late.

When he finally got to Dottie's house, he studied her front step.

"Did your mother move your pumpkin?" Leon asked.

"No," Dottie said. She shook her head hard, tossing her long, brown, wavy hair.

"What about Ginger?" Casey asked. Casey wore her straight blond hair in two braids.

"Maybe Ginger hid the pumpkin in a bush," Casey said.

Ginger was Dottie's cat.

"No." Dottie shook her head again. "It was too big for Ginger to move."

Dottie took a small notebook out of her back pocket. She carried her notebook everywhere. Inside, she kept lists. Her favorite was of the weather. Today, her weather list said, is sixty-nine degrees and sunny.

Dottie turned to the page where she listed measurements.

"My pumpkin weighed twenty-one pounds," Dottie reported.

"It was the biggest one," Leon said.

Leon had helped Dottie pick out the pumpkin at her uncle's store, which was a short walk from her house. Uncle Eddy sold flowers, vegetables, fruit, pie, and bread. In October, he sold pumpkins.

The pumpkin Dottie picked was the very best one. Everyone at the store agreed.

"Are you sure the pumpkin was here last night?" Casey asked. "Was it here when you woke up? Did you hear anything strange while you slept?"

Some people thought Casey asked too many questions. But Dottie and Leon were used to it.

"I heard the usual noises," Dottie said. She opened her book and started reading.

"Ginger's collar clinked when she came upstairs. Someone went to the bathroom and slammed the door. My brother's dumb alarm clock went off too early."

Sometimes when Dottie made lists, they were very long. So Leon interrupted her.

"You can see exactly where the pumpkin was," Leon said. He pointed to a perfect wet circle where the pumpkin used to be.

"Did someone steal it?" Casey asked.

All three heads turned toward the ivy-covered house across the street.

The house was dark. It looked like no one was home. They'd never met the woman who lived there because she traveled a lot. But they all felt the same way. The woman in the mysterious house might just be the type to steal a pumpkin.

CHAPTER TWO

THE FIRST CASE

"I DON'T LIKE that house," Dottie said.

"Neither do I," Leon agreed.

"I have an idea," Casey said. "Let's go to my backyard. My dad and I finally finished the clubhouse."

"I'm not in the mood," Dottie said.

"Not in the mood?" Casey said.

All summer long they had been talking about building a clubhouse. How could Dottie not want to see it?

"I have an idea," Casey tried again. "First we'll look at the clubhouse. Then we'll look for your pumpkin."

"Okay," Dottie said. She could never pass up the chance to do something first. "But first it's time for Ginger's walk."

Even though Ginger was a cat, she liked going for walks. That was because Ginger was a cat that thought she was a dog.

Casey had a dog that thought he was a cat. Casey's dog, Silky, liked to sit in front of the window and watch people walk by.

Leon didn't have a pet. He had allergies. So he collected rocks and other things instead. He also had curly hair and freckles on his nose. His mother said his freckles gave him personality. She said one day he'd wake up and be glad he had freckles. But that hadn't happened yet.

Dottie came out of her house holding the end of Ginger's leash. She let Ginger lead the way to Casey's house.

As they walked, Dottie counted. She'd always wondered how many footsteps it took to get to Casey's house. Twenty-nine footsteps, she wrote in her notebook.

Twenty-one more steps and they were in

Casey's backyard. She wrote that down, too.

Dottie put away her notebook and looked for Leon. He had been right behind her. Now he was nowhere to be seen. This was nothing new.

"Leon," Dottie called.

"Leon!" Casey yelled.

They heard the sound of Leon's sneakers on the gravel driveway.

"I found it," he said, rushing to join them.

"Where was it?" Casey asked. "Is it smashed? Is it broken? Is it carved?"

"What are you talking about?" Leon asked.

"The pumpkin!" Casey and Dottie said together.

"Oh," Leon said. "I didn't find the pumpkin. I found this."

Leon opened up his hand. Inside was a flat gray rock.

This was nothing new either.

"That's a really nice one," Dottie said.

"What is it?" Casey asked.

"Texas," Leon said. "Isn't it perfect?"

Casey and Dottie nodded. But to them it just looked like a funny-shaped rock.

Leon put the rock in his pocket. "Where's the clubhouse?" he asked.

"This way," Casey said.

She led them down a narrow path between two tall hedges.

"Here we are," Casey said.

There it was—their new clubhouse.

Casey proudly pointed to the sign hanging above the door. It said THE CALENDAR CLUB.

"I hope you don't mind that I named the clubhouse after me, Casey Calendar."

Dottie minded, but just a little.

"And you are the first and only members."

Dottie stopped minding. She liked that she and Leon were the first and only members.

Dottie walked into the clubhouse first, with Ginger right behind her.

"It's perfect," Dottie said.

Casey came in next.

"I think so, too," Casey said.

They looked at the door, waiting for Leon.

"Leon!" Casey shouted after a minute.

They heard the sound of rocks dropping to the ground. Then Leon ran inside.

"I almost forgot to tell you," he said. "On my way over here I saw Mrs. List, and guess what?"

Mrs. List was a teacher at the Fruitvale Elementary School. She lived two houses down from Leon.

"What?" Casey said.

"Mrs. List told me that her pumpkin disappeared, too."

Casey was about to ask a dozen questions. But a distant sound of music stopped her.

"What is that?" Casey asked.

"It sounds familiar," Dottie said.

"I know what it is," Leon said. "It's that song, 'Halloween Is Coming By.' We learned it back in kindergarten. Remember?"

They ran to the sidewalk just in time to see a truck drive by. It was the size of an ice-cream truck but painted bright orange.

There was a speaker on top of the truck. It was playing the Halloween song.

They watched as the truck slowed to a stop in front of Warren Bunn's house.

Warren Bunn was a boy in their grade. He scared almost everyone, and not just on Halloween! Warren Bunn was a bully and proud of it.

Casey, Dottie, and Leon crouched behind a big oak tree. They watched as Warren Bunn's mother talked to the truck driver. She handed over some money. The man handed over a pumpkin.

"Uncle Eddy told me about him," Dottie said. "He's the Pumpkin Man. He sells pumpkins from his truck. And he sells them cheaper than my uncle can."

"I'm sure his pumpkins aren't as big as your pumpkin," Leon said.

Dottie frowned. "What pumpkin?" she asked.

The three friends sat down on the curb.

"I wonder where my pumpkin could be," Dottie said.

Ginger stared, blinked, and rubbed herself against Dottie's leg to cheer her up.

Warren Bunn rode by on his bicycle, dragging his foot to slow down.

"Hey," Warren shouted. "What's the matter with all of you?" He didn't wait for an answer. "Someone steal your pumpkins?"

The three friends stood up at once as Warren rode away, laughing.

"Do you think Warren took your pumpkin?" Casey asked.

"Maybe," Dottie said.

"Or it could have been the woman in the ivy-covered house," Leon said.

Casey said, "It sounds to me like the Calendar Club just got its first case."

"Our first case," Dottie said. And for the first time all day, she smiled.

CHAPTER THREE
MORE GONE!

"I WONDER if they have pumpkins in Texas," Leon said.

Casey and Dottie looked at each other. Leon was going to be talking about Texas all day.

"I know the state bird is a mockingbird," Leon said. "And the capital is Austin. But I don't know if they grow pumpkins."

TEXAS

AUSTIN

"Leon," Casey said, "do you live in Texas or in New Jersey? Do you want to go to Austin, or do you want to go to Uncle Eddy's store to get Dottie and Mrs. List their new pumpkins?"

"Let's go to the store," Leon said.

Casey smiled. "Good idea."

Casey got her red wagon from the garage so they wouldn't have to carry the heavy pumpkins home. Then the three friends set off for the store.

Dottie led the way, walking Ginger.

Casey followed, pulling the wagon.

Leon was last. He stopped to pick up a rock, examined it, and tossed it back in the street. He stopped again to pick up another.

Leon had fallen half a block behind when he called out, "Hey! Look at this!"

"Which state do you think he found this time?" Casey asked Dottie as they walked back to Leon.

When they caught up to Leon, he opened his hand. But this time Casey and Dottie didn't see a rock.

"What is that?" Casey asked.

"A pumpkin stem," Leon said. "I found it here, on the ground."

The three friends looked from the ground to the nearest house. But there was no pumpkin on the steps of the house.

They looked across the street. There were no pumpkins there, either.

"Come on," Casey said. She walked up the front path of the nearest house and rang the bell.

"What are you doing?" Dottie asked.

"Mrs. Foust lives here," Casey said. "I'm going to find out if that stem belongs to her."

Leon put the stem in his pocket.

Mrs. Foust opened the door. "Hello, everyone," she said.

"Hello, Mrs. Foust," said the three friends.

"Mrs. Foust," Casey said, "did you buy your pumpkin yet?"

"Of course," Mrs. Foust said. "I bought it from Dottie's uncle."

"Is it in your backyard?" Casey asked.

Mrs. Foust laughed. "No. It's right outside, sitting on the top step."

Casey shook her head. Dottie shook her head. Leon shook his head.

"I'm sorry to tell you this," Casey said, "but it's not here."

Mrs. Foust came outside.

"But it was right there," she said when she saw her step.

"Hers is gone, too," Casey said, pointing to Dottie.

"So is Mrs. List's," Leon added.

Mrs. Foust looked up the block. "What happened to Mrs. MacGregor's pumpkin? She put a big one out yesterday afternoon."

Dottie took out her notebook. She wrote, Missing Pumpkins: Dottie Plum, Mrs. List, Mrs. Foust, and Mrs. MacGregor.

"I guess it's the same thing that happened to all the pumpkins," Casey said.

"We think someone stole them," Leon said. He looked toward Warren Bunn's house.

Mrs. Foust looked there, too. "Isn't that strange?" she said. "Mrs. Bunn is the only one on our street who still has a pumpkin."

"We just saw her buy it from the Pumpkin Man," Dottie explained.

"Oh, yes," Mrs. Foust said. "Your uncle told me about him." She looked at her front step and frowned. "I need a new pumpkin. But I'm not going to buy one from a truck. I'm going back to your uncle's store."

"That's where we're going now," Dottie said. "Would you like us to get you one?"

"That would be lovely," Mrs. Foust said. "But what I'd like even more is for you to find that pumpkin thief."

Casey, Dottie, and Leon agreed. That was exactly what they wanted, too.

The three friends continued up the street. Leon stopped to pick up stems he found on the ground. By the time they got to Uncle Eddy's store, his pockets were filled with pumpkin stems.

CHAPTER FOUR
THE EMPTY BENCH

"THAT'S ALL I've got left," Uncle Eddy said.

Dottie, Leon, and Casey stared at the three small, painted pumpkins on the long wooden bench.

"Are those the ones you painted?" Casey asked Dottie.

Dottie nodded. It was the first year Uncle Eddy agreed to let Dottie paint some of the

24

pumpkins. Leon had painted some, too.

Leon painted pumpkins with scary faces. His pumpkins had angry eyebrows and scowling mouths.

Dottie painted pumpkins with goofy faces. Her pumpkins had mouths with tongues hanging out and eyes that looked surprised.

Now all that remained were three small, goofy-faced pumpkins. Dottie thought the pumpkins looked lonely.

"Where are Leon's scary ones?" Casey asked.

"I sold them," Uncle Eddy said.

"I guess the scary ones sold better," Dottie said.

"No." Uncle Eddy smiled. "I had yours over near the apple bins as decoration. I just moved them back to the bench a few minutes ago. They're all I have left."

Dottie looked at the bench. Yesterday, it had been crowded with pumpkins. There were tall ones, short ones, fat ones, and skinny ones. There were lumpy ones, long-stemmed ones, and a couple that had big dents. How could there only be three small pumpkins left?

"I get the same amount every year because I know how many customers I have," Uncle Eddy explained. "But I didn't plan on pumpkins going missing and people coming back to buy more.

"Over a dozen little kids came here crying this morning," Uncle Eddy said. "They were sad that their pumpkins are gone. I feel terrible about it. And so do the police."

"The police?" Casey said. "Who called the police?"

"I did," Uncle Eddy answered.

He took the remaining three pumpkins off the bench.

"I saved the ones you painted," he told Dottie. "I want you to have them."

Uncle Eddy loaded the painted pumpkins into Casey's red wagon. Then he sat down on the empty bench where the pumpkins used to be. He looked sadder than Dottie had ever seen him.

"I guess I'm glad the Pumpkin Man came to Fruitvale this October after all," Uncle Eddy said. "I wish I knew where to find him. I've got some customers I'd like to send his way."

"We saw him today," Dottie said. "He came to our street and sold a pumpkin to Mrs. Bunn."

Uncle Eddy reached into his back pocket and pulled out a piece of paper. "If you see him again, tell him I've got new customers for him."

Dottie took out her notebook. "Can I copy down the list?"

Uncle Eddy nodded and handed over the paper.

Dottie started copying the names into her notebook.

"We can find the Pumpkin Man for you," Casey said. "And with the names in Dottie's notebook, we can tell him exactly where to go."

"Would you do that?" Uncle Eddy asked.

The three friends nodded.

"That's great," Uncle Eddy said. "And while you're at it, maybe you can find the pumpkin thief, too."

CHAPTER FIVE
WARREN'S BACKYARD

THEY STOPPED at Mrs. Foust's house first. This time Dottie rang the bell.

"These painted pumpkins were all Uncle Eddy had left," Dottie said.

She handed Mrs. Foust a pumpkin.

"Thank you," Mrs. Foust said. "It's a lovely pumpkin. It has such a nice face." She admired the pumpkin's silly grin.

"This one goes to Mrs. List," Dottie said as they made their way down the block.

Mrs. List wasn't home. So Dottie tore out a piece of paper from the back of her book and wrote a note.

Dear Mrs. List,
This is the only pumpkin my uncle had left.
From, Dottie Plum

Dottie put a pumpkin on the front step and stuck the note in the mail slot.

Leon put the last pumpkin on Dottie's step. Just then, Warren and his best friend, Derek, rode up on their bikes.

"Knock, knock," Warren called.

"Who's there," Derek yelled back.

"Waa, waa," Warren said.

"Waa, waa, who?" Derek asked.

"Waa, waa. Someone took my pumpkin and gave me an ugly-faced one instead!"

Warren and Derek rode off, laughing.

Casey, Dottie, and Leon glared.

"Maybe we should look in Warren Bunn's backyard," Casey said.

"For my missing pumpkin?" Dottie asked.

"For all the missing pumpkins," Leon said.

Dottie put Ginger back in the house. Then the three friends walked up the street to where Warren Bunn lived.

They ran up the driveway into his backyard.

They found Warren Bunn's little sister, Emma, sitting on a blanket on the patio. She was playing with dolls.

Leon and Dottie froze.

Casey smiled. "Hi, Emma," she said.

Emma said, "Hi."

Emma was four. "What are you doing in my backyard?" Emma asked.

"We're looking for pumpkins," Casey said.

"Oh," Emma said. "We have a pumpkin. We got it from the Pumpkin Man."

"Does your brother have lots of pumpkins?" Casey asked. "Does he keep pumpkins in the garage? Or in his room?"

Emma laughed. "You're silly. Why would he keep pumpkins in the garage?"

Mrs. Bunn looked out through the kitchen window.

"Emma," she called, "who are you talking to?"

"Casey Calendar," Emma called back. "She's looking for pumpkins."

Mrs. Bunn came outside. "I heard about the missing pumpkins," she said. "I think it's just terrible."

"We're trying to find out who took them," Dottie explained.

"Well, I hope you do," Mrs. Bunn said. "We're lucky. It looks like our pumpkin is the only one left."

"We got it from the Pumpkin Man," Emma told them again.

"We're looking for the Pumpkin Man," Dottie said.

"He's coming back here," Mrs. Bunn said. "He told Mrs. Tunnell, across the street, he'd have some nice pumpkins for her later today. She wants four," Mrs. Bunn told them. "One for each of her children to carve."

"If you see the Pumpkin Man, can you

tell him we're looking for him?" Casey asked.

"Of course, Casey," said Mrs. Bunn.

As Casey, Dottie, and Leon walked down the driveway, they wondered how someone like Warren Bunn could have such a nice mother.

When they got to the sidewalk, they heard the faint sound of music.

"That is so familiar," Dottie said. "Where have I heard that before?"

"It's the Pumpkin Man," Leon said.

Casey said, "Let's go."

The three friends took off to find him.

CHAPTER SIX
THE PUMPKIN MAN

"WAIT A MINUTE," Casey said.

Dottie and Leon stopped. They were in front of the scary ivy-covered house. There was a low iron fence around the house. The older kids in the neighborhood liked to sit on the fence in the dark to tell ghost stories.

Leon, Dottie, and Casey liked ghost stories. But they did not like to be in front of the ivy-covered house, even during the day.

"We should get going," Dottie said.

Leon nodded.

"Wait," Casey said. "Look."

Dottie and Leon looked.

"Look in the window," Casey said.

Dottie and Leon looked in the window.

A big round pumpkin looked back at them.

The pumpkin was carved. It had a toothy

smile, slits for eyes, and a triangle nose.

"The eyes are flickering," Leon said.

"That's because there's a candle inside," Dottie explained, hoping she was right.

"Does that pumpkin look familiar?" Casey asked. "Could that pumpkin be yours?"

Dottie stared hard.

"Isn't it fat like yours was?" Casey asked. "Isn't it as big as yours was? Didn't yours—" Casey stopped. "Listen," she said.

They heard music. It was getting louder.

"It's the Pumpkin Man," Casey said.

They ran, following the music.

"There he is!" Leon said, pointing to the orange truck.

The truck was stopped in front of a house. The three friends walked up to it.

A woman was handing money to the Pumpkin Man.

"Do you have anything that's a little more round?" the woman asked.

Dottie, Casey, and Leon looked at the pumpkin in her arms. It was tall, thin, and funny looking.

"That's all I have left for now," the Pumpkin Man said. "But I can stop by tomorrow. I'll have some more then."

"That's all right," the woman said. "This one is kind of cute."

She noticed Dottie, Casey, and Leon. "Do you think it's cute?" she asked.

They nodded politely.

She smiled. "You've got some more customers," the woman told the Pumpkin Man. She carried her tall, skinny pumpkin into her house.

When the Pumpkin Man saw the three friends, he smiled. His eyes crinkled.

"Good afternoon," the Pumpkin Man said. "What can I do for you today?"

"You're the Pumpkin Man, right?" Casey asked.

"That's me," said the Pumpkin Man.
"And this is my truck."

"We're glad we found you," Leon said.
He pointed to Dottie. "Dottie's uncle sells
pumpkins, just like you do."

The Pumpkin Man looked surprised and a
little annoyed. "Oh."

"Except he doesn't have any more
pumpkins," Dottie said. "Because someone's
been stealing pumpkins all around town.
And now his customers are really upset.

Some are even crying."

"The little kids," Leon explained.

"Her uncle wants to know if you could help him," Casey said.

"Oh," the Pumpkin Man said. He didn't sound annoyed anymore.

"Uncle Eddy has lots of customers who need pumpkins," Dottie said. "Could you sell them some of yours?"

She took her notebook out of her pocket. "I haven't finished copying all the addresses down. But I've got some of them written right here."

The Pumpkin Man smiled. "I'd be happy to help. I'm all out of pumpkins right now. But I'll have more tomorrow. I can stop by your house then if you like."

"Okay," Dottie said.

The Halloween song suddenly started to play. The Pumpkin Man leaned over and banged on the switch.

The three friends stared.

He banged the switch again.

The music stopped.

"That's better," the Pumpkin Man said. "This sound system is pretty old. It doesn't work the way it's supposed to anymore."

"What's wrong with it?" Casey asked.

"Guess you could say it's moody," the Pumpkin Man explained with a laugh. "Sometimes when I turn the thing on, nothing happens."

Suddenly the music started up again.

The Pumpkin Man smiled. "Other times, it just starts up by itself."

He fiddled with the switch and gave it one more bang. The music stopped.

"Just a small electrical problem," he said. "No reason to worry." And he drove away.

"He's a nice man," Casey said.

"I don't know," Dottie said. There was

something about him that bothered her, but she couldn't explain it.

Leon spied another pumpkin stem on the sidewalk. He picked it up.

"Let's go back to the clubhouse and think about this," Casey said.

When Casey and Dottie got back to the clubhouse, Leon was nowhere to be seen. This was nothing new.

CHAPTER SEVEN

BLUE PUMPKINS

THE NEXT day, Dottie took out the list her uncle had given her. "Here are all the names and addresses of everyone whose pumpkin is gone," she said.

"Do the people have anything in common?" Casey asked. "Is there any kind of connection or pattern?"

"The only pattern I see is that pumpkins are missing from practically every street in Fruitvale," Dottie said.

Leon came bursting into the clubhouse. "Look what I found!"

"Florida?" Dottie asked, because Leon had been talking about looking for a rock shaped like Florida all summer.

"No," Leon said.

He carefully placed a pumpkin stem in the middle of the floor.

"Look at this pumpkin stem," Leon said. "It's different."

Dottie and Casey squatted down beside the stem. They looked as hard as they could.

"It's a long stem," Dottie said.

"And curvy," Casey said.

"And the very top of it looks like it's painted black," Dottie said. "Uncle Eddy does that. He color codes the pumpkin stems so he knows how much to charge for them. I wrote that down somewhere."

She opened her notebook. "Here it is," she said after she found the right page. "Black-tipped ones weigh five to ten pounds."

"Look at the bottom of the stem," Leon said.

Dottie picked up the stem to examine it more closely.

"The bottom of it is perfectly flat,"

Black-tipped ones weigh five to ten pounds.

Dottie said. "It looks like it was cut straight across with a knife."

She handed the stem to Casey.

Casey examined it. "Are all the stems cut just like this one?" she asked.

"Yes," Leon said. "Look at this one." He held up another stem.

The girls stood up and looked closer.

Leon pointed to the wide bottom of the stem and said, "Look here."

Dottie saw it first. "It's blue," she said.

Casey saw it, too. There was a thin blue line at the bottom of the stem.

"Could there be such a thing as a blue

pumpkin?" Casey asked. "I've never heard of a blue pumpkin."

"I have," Leon said.

"Where?" Casey asked. "Don't tell me. Are there blue pumpkins in Texas?"

"No!" Dottie said. "But there are in Fruitvale!"

"Where?" Casey asked again.

"Leon painted a blue pumpkin at Uncle Eddy's store," Dottie said. "I remember because I got mad."

"Why?" Casey asked.

"Uncle Eddy bought only one jar of every color paint," Dottie explained.

"And I used up all the blue paint on the first pumpkin I painted," Leon said.

"It was that exact blue," Dottie said, pointing to the stem.

"So that means this stem came from Leon's blue pumpkin," Casey said.

Leon nodded. "I think after someone

bought my pumpkin, someone stole it."

"This is our big break," Casey said. "How hard could it be to find a blue pumpkin?"

"It could be pretty hard," Dottie said.

"Why?" Casey said.

Dottie turned to Leon. "Remember the paint we used?"

"Oh," Leon said. "Right. I forgot."

"Forgot what?" Casey asked.

"It was the first time Uncle Eddy let us paint his pumpkins," Dottie said. "That's why he didn't know."

"Didn't know what?" Casey asked.

"That he bought washable paint," Dottie said.

"So someone could have stolen my pumpkin," Leon said, "and then washed off the blue paint."

Casey sighed. "Why would someone go to all that trouble?"

Before anyone could answer, they heard the Halloween song again.

"He's back!" Leon said.

They ran to the sidewalk. The pumpkin truck was waiting for them.

The Pumpkin Man stuck his head out of the door on the side of the truck.

"Got that list for me?" he asked.

Dottie took out her notebook. She had her uncle's list still tucked inside. But she hadn't finished copying all the names yet.

"I can give you the first page now," she said. She handed over the first page of the list her uncle had given her. "I'll have the rest copied by the end of the day if you want to come back for it."

"Okay," the Pumpkin Man said, sounding disappointed. "I guess it's a start."

He closed the door and drove away. The Halloween song stopped, then started, then stopped again. They could hear the

Pumpkin Man yelling about the broken switch as he drove away.

"Wait a minute," Dottie said. "I know why that song's familiar."

"It's because we all learned it in kindergarten," Leon insisted.

"No," Dottie said. She looked up and down the street.

"Let's go back to the clubhouse," Dottie said. "I'll tell you there."

CHAPTER EIGHT
DOTTIE REMEMBERS

WHEN THEY got back to the clubhouse, Leon laid out the pumpkin stems on the floor. He sorted them according to height.

"Look at this," Leon said.

The girls looked.

Leon pointed to a stem. "That's the one with the blue paint," he said. He pointed to another. "This one has red paint."

"Didn't you paint red hair on one of the pumpkins?" Dottie asked.

Leon nodded.

"And this one—" He pointed to the third stem.

"Why does that one have all different colors?" Casey asked.

"I remember that one," Dottie said. "That was the last pumpkin you painted,"

Dottie said to Leon. "You gave that one rainbow hair."

Leon nodded again, happy that Dottie remembered.

"You found all three stems you painted," Casey said.

Leon nodded once more.

"That means that someone stole all your painted pumpkins," Casey said. "But we still don't know why."

"I have an idea," Dottie said. She opened her notebook. "Listen to this."

The three friends all sat on the floor cross-legged.

Dottie read aloud. "Ginger's collar clinked when she came upstairs."

"I know what that is," Leon said. "That's your list of the sounds you heard the night your pumpkin was stolen."

"Right," Dottie said. "At first I thought Ginger's collar clinking was a normal sound.

There are two tags on Ginger's collar and, when she walks, they clink and jingle and make a lot of noise. Except then I realized Ginger doesn't walk around at night."

Dottie read on. "Someone went to the bathroom and slammed the door. My brother's dumb alarm clock went off too early."

"Wait a minute," Casey said. "Don't alarm clocks go off at the same time every morning? Isn't that the point of an alarm clock?"

Dottie's eyes got bigger. "That's what I was thinking. Then I remembered that I looked at *my* clock when I heard my brother's alarm go off. It was three in the morning."

"In the middle of the night," Leon said.

"Exactly," Dottie said. She whispered the next part. "Now I realize it wasn't Jack's alarm clock I heard at all. I thought it was his because he has it set so the music comes on really loud. But today when I heard the music from the pumpkin truck, I realized why that song was so familiar. It was the Halloween song that I heard at three in the morning!"

"You heard the pumpkin truck," Leon said.

Dottie nodded. "Remember what the Pumpkin Man told us about his sound system?"

"He said it's broken," Casey said. "He said it always goes off when he doesn't want it to."

"Like in the middle of the night," Leon said.

Dottie nodded.

"But why would the Pumpkin Man drive around in the middle of the night?" Casey asked. "Why would he try to sell pumpkins when everyone is asleep?"

"Because maybe he wasn't really *selling* pumpkins," Dottie said.

"Maybe he was *stealing* pumpkins," Leon said. "Your pumpkin."

The three friends sat perfectly still.

"Why would he do that?" Casey asked. "Unless—" She thought a moment. "Unless he stole the pumpkins in the night—"

Dottie finished her sentence, "and sold them in the morning!"

CHAPTER NINE

CALLING OFFICER GILL

WHEN THEY got to Uncle Eddy's store, they found him restocking the apple bins.

"Aren't these Golden Delicious apples beautiful?" Uncle Eddy asked. He carefully added six shiny yellow apples to the top of a bin.

"Those are my favorite kind," Leon said.

Uncle Eddy smiled and handed Leon a Golden Delicious apple. He handed Dottie a red McIntosh, because he knew those were her favorite.

"What about you?" Uncle Eddy asked Casey. "What kind of apple are you in the mood for?"

"I'd like a Granny Smith, please," Casey said, pointing to the green apples. "And we'd like to tell you what we figured out."

"Okay," Uncle Eddy said. "Let's sit down and have a talk while we eat our apples."

Uncle Eddy was a big believer in taking time out to eat healthy snacks.

He took a Red Delicious out of a bin and followed the children to the empty pumpkin bench. They all sat down.

"Did you get a chance to talk to the Pumpkin Man yet?" Uncle Eddy asked. He took a big bite of his juicy apple.

Dottie took a big bite of hers and nodded.

"We did. But he's not who you think he is," Casey said. She took a bite of her Granny Smith.

"He's not a man who sells pumpkins out

of a truck?" Uncle Eddy asked.

"He does sell pumpkins out of his truck," Leon said.

"But do you know where he gets his pumpkins?" Casey asked.

Uncle Eddy thought a minute. "I get mine from a pumpkin farm here in New Jersey. I can't say what farm he gets his from. There are pumpkin farms all across the United States, as far away as Texas."

Leon smiled. "I always wondered if pumpkins grew in Texas!"

"We'll talk about Texas later," Casey said. "After we finish telling Uncle Eddy about the pumpkin thief."

"I thought we were talking about the Pumpkin Man," Uncle Eddy said.

"Same person!" Dottie said.

Casey and Leon nodded.

"What do you mean?" Uncle Eddy asked.

"We figured it out," Dottie said.

"The Pumpkin Man sells pumpkins in the morning," Casey said.

Leon told the rest. "But he gets them by stealing them at night."

As soon as Uncle Eddy finished his apple, he called the police.

Officer Gill was at the store in less than five minutes.

He pulled his notebook out of his back pocket.

Dottie pulled hers out of her back pocket.

"Nice notebook," Officer Gill told Dottie.

"I like yours, too," Dottie told Officer Gill.

The three friends told Officer Gill their story. He wrote everything down. So did Dottie.

"I'll have a talk with this Pumpkin Man," Officer Gill said. "But I'm afraid I can't charge him with any crime."

"Why not?" Casey asked. "Isn't it against the law to steal pumpkins? Shouldn't he go to jail?"

Officer Gill laughed. "If he stole those pumpkins, he'll go to jail. But we don't have any proof. At least not yet."

Officer Gill put his notebook back in his pocket. Then he got in his car and drove off to look for the Pumpkin Man.

"How is he going to find proof?" Leon asked.

"I have an idea," Casey said. "And all we need is a nice big pumpkin."

"I'm afraid I can't help you there," Uncle Eddy said.

Dottie smiled. "But I can."

CHAPTER TEN
GOTCHA!

"**WE JUST** need to borrow it overnight,"
Dottie explained to Mrs. Bunn.

"Do you still think that my brother is a
pumpkin stealer?" Emma asked, poking her
head out from behind her mother.

Mrs. Bunn looked at the children sternly.
"Is that what you think?"

"No, Mrs. Bunn," Leon said.

"But some people might," Casey said.
"That's why we need your pumpkin to
prove who the pumpkin thief is."

Just then Warren Bunn and Derek rode
their bikes into the driveway.

"Hello, Warren," Mrs. Bunn said. "Hello,
Derek."

"Hello, Mrs. Bunn," Derek said.

"Warren," Mrs. Bunn said, "your bicycle
helmet won't do your head any good if it's

hanging on your handlebars."

"I know, Mom," Warren said.

He looked at Leon, Casey, and Dottie.

"What are they doing here?" Warren asked.

"They're here to prove you're not a pumpkin thief," Emma said as her mother handed their big fat pumpkin to Casey.

"Hey," Warren said. "Mommy, that's my pumpkin."

Dottie, Casey, and Leon thought it sounded funny to hear Warren say "Mommy." But they didn't laugh. They just hurried up the block to Casey's backyard.

When they got to the clubhouse, Leon and Casey held the pumpkin upside down. Dottie got the paintbrush, because Dottie had the best handwriting.

Using waterproof paint, Dottie carefully wrote the word GOTCHA on the bottom of the pumpkin.

Casey called her dad to take a look.

"You're our witness," Casey told him. "Can you read what it says on the bottom?"

"Gotcha," read Casey's dad.

"Can you describe the color of the paint?" Casey asked.

"Purple," said Casey's dad.

"Thanks, Dad," Casey said.

"Any time," Casey's dad said.

They put the big pumpkin in the red wagon and carted it over to Dottie's house.

Dottie's mother came outside just as they were putting it on the front step.

"You found your pumpkin," Dottie's mother said.

Dottie looked at the pumpkin again. It did look like her pumpkin.

"I don't think you should get too attached to it, Mrs. Plum," Leon said. "We don't think it will be here in the morning."

CHAPTER ELEVEN

FOUND IT!

THAT NIGHT the three friends tried to stay up and listen for the pumpkin truck. But the activities of the day had tired them out, and they were all asleep by nine o'clock.

Dottie woke up first the next morning. She ran downstairs and swung open her front door.

"It's gone!" she yelled out.

Casey and Leon heard her yell.

"It *is* gone," they said when they arrived together, minutes later.

Dottie's mother called Officer Gill.

Officer Gill agreed to let the children ride with him in his police car to look for the stolen pumpkin.

Dottie was the one who saw it first.

"Over there," she said. She pointed to a small house. On the top step was a big, perfect pumpkin.

"That's it," she said. "I'm sure of it."

The children ran out of the car. They turned the pumpkin over.

Officer Gill followed right behind. He read the word writtten on the bottom of the pumpkin: GOTCHA.

Officer Gill pressed his lips together. He looked angry. He rang the bell.

"Coming," a voice called. The door swung open.

An elderly woman smiled politely. "Can I help you?"

"Good morning, Mrs. Miller," Officer Gill said. "Can you tell me where you got this beautiful pumpkin?"

"Of course," Mrs. Miller said. "First I went to Dottie's uncle's store. But he was all out. And my grandchildren are coming tomorrow night for our annual Halloween pumpkin-carving party. We do it every year."

Casey, who wasn't as patient as Officer Gill, interrupted. "What we need to know is, where did you get this pumpkin?"

"I really did try your uncle first," Mrs. Miller explained to Dottie again.

"It's all right," Dottie said. "Uncle Eddy understands."

"That looks like a very heavy pumpkin," Leon said.

"I know," Mrs. Miller said. "That's why I feel so lucky that the Pumpkin Man came to our street. He was here bright and early. And he carried the pumpkin right to my front door. Only charged me ten dollars for it, too."

"Thank you, Mrs. Miller," Officer Gill said. "I'm afraid I'll have to ask you not to carve this pumpkin. Evidence," he explained.

"If you don't mind a painted one, I can give you mine for your grandkids to carve," Dottie offered.

"That's very kind of you," Mrs. Miller said. "But I think we'll do something else this year. Maybe we'll make candy apples. Everyone loves candy apples, right?"

The three friends nodded. They loved candy apples.

"We've got to be on our way," Officer Gill said. "There's an orange-colored truck I have to find."

"I'll drop you all at home," Officer Gill told Leon, Dottie, and Casey.

"Can't we go with you?" Leon asked.

"Sorry. I'm afraid not," Officer Gill said. "That wouldn't be safe."

Officer Gill drove to Dottie's house. The three friends were about to get out of his car when they heard the music.

"He's coming," Dottie whispered.

Officer Gill pulled his car up Dottie's driveway. He drove to the back of Dottie's house, so his car couldn't be seen from the street.

The Pumpkin Man parked in front.

The children went to meet him.

"Do you have the rest of that list for me?" the Pumpkin Man asked.

"Yes," Dottie said. "Now, where did I put it?"

"Come on," the Pumpkin Man said. "I don't have all day."

"I've got the list right here," a voice called from up the driveway.

The Pumpkin Man rushed past the children to see who had the list. He wasn't expecting to find Officer Gill waiting for him.

"Thank you, Dottie," Officer Gill said as he led the Pumpkin Man to his police car. "Thank you, Leon. Thank you, Casey. You all did a great job."

The three friends watched as Officer Gill drove away with the Pumpkin Man. Then they walked over to Mrs. Bunn's house to explain what happened to her pumpkin.

When Mrs. Bunn went inside to tell
Emma and Warren, the three friends heard
what sounded like someone crying.

Warren came out of the house. His eyes
looked red. His nose was running.
He wiped it on his sleeve.

"Sorry about your pumpkin,"
Dottie said.

"Who cares about a
pumpkin?" Warren said.
"And what are you staring
at?" he asked Leon.

"Nothing," Leon said. He
looked at the ground. "I'm just
looking for rocks."

"Who cares about rocks?" Warren said.

"We do," Casey answered. And the
three friends hurried home.

CHAPTER TWELVE

PUMPKIN PARTY

DOTTIE, CASEY, and Leon put flyers all around town.

CELEBRATE HALLOWEEN
AT EDDY'S STORE!
Saturday Morning 11 a.m.
Cider! Donuts! Apples! Lots of pumpkins!

Uncle Eddy beamed as he led his neighbors to shelves filled with pumpkins.

Officer Gill had found the rest of the stolen pumpkins in a field just outside of town. It only took Uncle Eddy one trip to take them back to the store in his truck.

Uncle Eddy didn't charge anyone for the pumpkins this time. He said he didn't believe in selling the same thing twice.

"Don't you have to keep the pumpkins as evidence?" Casey asked Officer Gill as she passed around a tray of donuts.

"I only need to keep one," Officer Gill said as he took a bite of a cider donut, which was his favorite kind. "So I kept my own!"

Some people tried to find the pumpkin they started out with. Other people took whatever pumpkin they saw first.

The only one who seemed unhappy was Warren Bunn.

"Ours was bigger than this," Warren complained as his mother picked up a small pumpkin with some blue paint on the top.

Uncle Eddy climbed up on a crate to make an announcement.

"Can I have your attention?" he called out.

The crowd quieted.

"I'd like to thank my niece, Dottie Plum," Uncle Eddy said. "And her friends, Leon Spector and Casey Calendar."

Everyone cheered.

Dottie beamed. She loved being thanked first.

"They've done a great job," Officer Gill

added. "It turns out that the Pumpkin Man has run this scam in six other states."

"Which states?" Leon called out.

Officer Gill didn't hear him. "Thanks to our young detectives, he's now behind bars where he belongs."

The crowd cheered again.

Dottie, Leon, and Casey smiled their biggest smiles. Then Casey got up on a crate next to Officer Gill.

Dottie and Leon looked at each other. They had no idea what Casey was going to say.

"Does anyone else have any mysteries that need to be solved?" Casey asked. "If you do, you can leave a note in the Calendar Club 'Help Box.' I put the box outside our clubhouse door."

"How did you figure out who did it?" asked a little voice. It was Emma Bunn.

"You can read all about that in our newspaper, *The Monthly Calendar*," Casey said.

She looked over at Dottie and Leon. "I hope you don't mind," she said, "but I named it after me."

Dottie minded, but just a little.

"And the first issue," Casey told the crowd, "will be written by our star reporter, Dottie Plum."

Dottie smiled, happy she was going to write the first issue.

"It's time for each of you to take home a pumpkin," Uncle Eddy said. "And have a great time carving it!"

That's exactly what everyone did. And Dottie carved hers first.

The Monthly Calendar

~~~~~~ Issue One • Volume One ~~~~~~

OCTOBER

Publisher: Casey Calendar
Editor: Dottie Plum
Fact Checker: Leon Spector

Calendar Club Cracks First Case!

THE BIG NEWS IN FRUITVALE this October was the disappearance of pumpkins all over town. Calendar Club members Casey Calendar, Dottie Plum, and Leon Spector followed the trail of pumpkin stems and strange sounds to figure out who the pumpkin thief was. To celebrate, Dottie's Uncle Eddy gave free pumpkins to all!

ASK LEON

Do you have a question about a state for Leon Spector? If you do, send it to him and he'll answer it for you.

Dear Leon,

Can pumpkins really grow in Texas? What else grows in Texas?

> From,
> I've Never Been to Texas
> But I Really Want to Go

Dear I've Never Been to Texas,

Yes, pumpkins do grow in Texas. Pecans and peaches also grow in Texas, (just to mention two other P words).

Other facts about Texas:

Texas is known as the Lone Star State.

The state flower is the bluebonnet.

The state bird is the mockingbird.

The state tree is the pecan tree.

The state motto is Friendship.

Your friend,

Leon

DOTTIE'S WEATHER BOX

In October,

it rained on 14 days.

It was cloudy on 10 days.

It was sunny on 7 days.

It was dark every night.

How many days are in October?

CALENDAR CLUB MYSTERIES™

The Case of the
MISSING PUMPKINS

by **NANCY STAR**

Illustrated by
JAMES BERNARDIN

SCHOLASTIC INC.

New York   Toronto   London   Auckland   Sydney
Mexico City   New Delhi   Hong Kong   Buenos Aires

To Izzy and Lizzy
—N. S.

To Lisa and Wyeth, for putting up with me
and the crazy schedule I keep!
—J. B.

*Special thanks to Ryan, Maddie, and Lissie
for being such wonderful models.*

ISBN 0-439-67260-0

Text copyright © 2004 by Nancy Star
Illustrations copyright © 2004 by James Bernardin
All rights reserved. Published by Scholastic Inc.

SCHOLASTIC and associated logos are trademarks
and/or registered trademarks of Scholastic Inc.

12 11 10 9 8 7 6 5 4 3 2 1   4 5 6 7 8 9/0

Printed in the U.S.A.   40
First printing, October 2004

Book design by Jennifer Rinaldi Windau